Papito y Chiquitita

PAPITO Y CHIQUITITA

poems and stories

C.G. Moro

Moro, C.G.

ISBN: 979-8-9891319-0-7

Edited by Belèn Lohr

Cover art by Nicholas Danger

Know Good Books

San Diego, CA

For every parent out there
still wondering when we may ever stop
feeling like kids ourselves.

Table of Contents

Papito

Aidan James

March 4th, 2007

2:00 AM

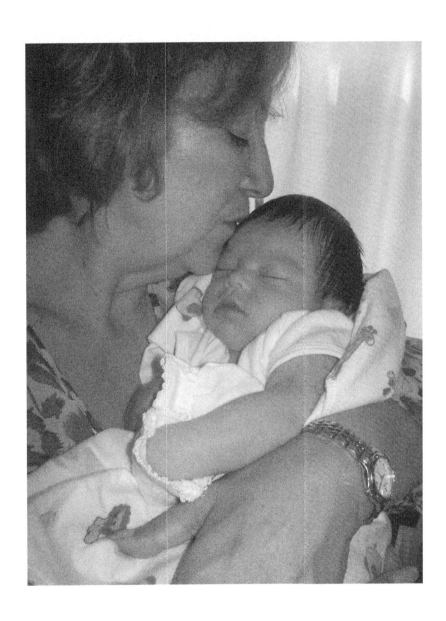

[the marlin and me]

I spent all year not knowing how old I am.

Not that I do not know what year I was born or what year it currently is but more that time has become a marlin in the vast blue ocean and I have been living in a tugboat pulling along a barge laden with all my brackish hopes and saline dreams towards a port eternally just over the horizon.

The ocean is vast.
I work every day.
The ocean is deep.
I work every day.
There are no tides out here.
There are no waves.

There is only the marlin and me.

I am 7 years old eating peaches in the crux of the old peach tree out back. I am 17, falling in love over and over. I am 37, a father figure still figuring it out.

I am the captain now. The fishing rods bob up and down as they troll behind the boat. A dorsal fin flashes off in the distance as the marlin reminds me it is still out there. I feel my age in my bones. Everything tastes of salt and tomorrow is such a long time.

Across the still water I hear my mom calling me in for dinner. The sun dips below the horizon and in the penumbra I see myself setting the table for our grandkids.

4

The marlin lives on.
As do I.

[more of us]

you have lots of hopes and dreams tied up in an unborn baby
years of what-ifs
could-have-beens
projections of a soul that is half your best self
and half the best self of the person you love the most

losing a baby is hard
because a baby centers you so
and to lose that centering force
leaves you off kilter
spinning a bit
topsy-turvy into your own issues and doubts

We lost Tristan Lee Moro on June 9, 2017.
that was hard
it helped to know that lots of families
go through something similar
helped to know we were not alien
or less than
or broken in some manner

there is a new joy making its way into our reality

more of us

And to speak of the new joy in the same breath as Tristan

is not meant to be morbid or dark

but rather a love-full acknowledgement

that we exist

and survive

and procreate

and love

beyond

I see the line of time

so clearly

from my ancestors

through me

to these tiny beings we are charged with

and I love that line

honor it

am thankful for it

I never knew it possible

to love this much

and feel this much hope

all at once.

[my son, 14]

I remember the small, rented room I sat in
the night I found out you were on your journey
to me.

I remember the chipped paint in one of the corners
where the drywall did not meet just so
and the old folk songs I listened to as I stared out the window
into the city lights.

I remember the weight of you in my mind.
the sense of responsibility and fear and excitement.
Heavy waves of the unknown and unknowable
crashing over me, over and over.

I remember the questions
loud and multitudinous
ringing out in my ears.
They were, as was most of my life to that point,
centered on me.

Could I be a good father?
Could I provide what is needed?
Would I be enough?

They were, I realize now,

                                      amalgamations of all my fears
                                       over the many years spent
                                        without a father and
                                         without direction.

I remember you
so small and in need of me
your tiny fingers barely able to grasp my pinky
your eyes searching and trusting.

I remember as your Abuela,
a fierce mujer who had made grown men tremble in her day,
melted into you.

I remember seeing the answer in your eyes
to all the questions I had.

I remember knowing that I was meant to be your father.
That I wasn't meant to merely provide
but to live and teach abundance and grace.

I remember knowing that not only was I enough
but I was made for this, made for you.

14 years have come and gone
and we are still learning each other.
Our family has grown and our sense of abundance

9

and grace has grown with it.

I wish for you to always see yourself
in the same light I see you in.
I wish for you the same sense of perspective
during the lows as during the highs.
I wish for you to always know that not only are you enough,

but you were made for this.

I wish you, Papito, a very happy birthday.

[bueno, bonito y barato]

"PANTALONES! PANTAAAAALONES!
Señoraseñor páselepáselepásele!
Uno por diez, dos por quince.
Hay de los buenos por aquí. Páselepáseleeee!"

The flea market is popping on Wednesday mornings. Everybody looking for a deal. My voice is hoarse from calling out to all the *señoras* and *señores* passing us by.

We got here before the sun. Our light blue Nissan pickup is loaded to the brim with second-hand 501 jeans from the Goodwill wholesaler.

Days spent rummaging through bins full of broken toys and deferred dreams. Pulling out anything even remotely salvageable.

My mom would stay up late in the garage with her novelas blaring on a tiny television, trimming and patching away. The burr of the commercial overlock machine a frequency I remembered from the womb. Her deft hand movements as she stitched and cross-stitched the night away were mesmerizing.

Some nights I would stay up with her para *chusmear*. We would meander from gossip to life advice as seamlessly as her patches. She would peer at me over her reading glasses and always have a saying that was just right for just right then.

We made a formidable team. She would find and fix the merchandise and I would make it my mission to talk to every single person that walked by our stall.

We were good.

Real good.

At one point the *viejos* from the other stalls that had been in business longer than us got mad. They thought we were cheating with our low prices and hated the buzz that surrounded our stall. They forced us out of the main avenue at the market where all the textile stalls were and had management put us out by the fruit vendors.

My mom was livid. She tried arguing with the manager but the *viejos* were his friends and he paid her no mind. We muddled through the day and barely covered our costs. The ride back home was quiet, but I could see the fire in my mom's eyes as she silently argued with the manager in her head. Her hand came slightly off the steering wheel as she gestured her disdain.

The next week we got there earlier than even the old security guard that unlocked the gate to the parking lot. I was half asleep as we set up our table and made sure to get our rightful spot.

We rented two stalls that day and my mom joined me in pitching to the sea of strangers. We tag teamed every sale. I would pull them in and she would close them. I could hear her cackling laugh behind me as she chatted with the customers and a line formed.

We were a force of nature. I buttered up every *doña* within earshot. Reminded them that their husband's birthday was probably coming up, that their kids would soon *"pegar un estirón"* and need new jeans. I was 12 maybe 13 at the time and did not know what failure or rejection was. That day we were gods among mere flea market mortals.

We sold out before 10AM. Everything. Every single jean, t-shirt, jacket, knick-knack. The fanny pack we used to hold our change was overflowing. My mom contemplated trekking back home to grab more merchandise but thought of a better idea.

We loaded our table and chairs onto the truck and called the manager over to let him know we had to leave. Usually, you have to wait for the crowds to die down before you can pack up, but we were done so early that my mom insisted.

The manager reluctantly had two of his workers help guide us out with their tiny orange flags in each hand. They directed us to turn left towards the nearest exit but my mom turned right.

"Que hacès, ma?" I questioned her but she just instructed me to roll down my window.

The workers followed our lead and cleared the path for us down the main drag. They didn't get paid enough to care or argue. We slowly made our way to the main exit and I suddenly realized what my mom was doing.

The crowd opened up before us and my mom rolled her window down too. She made sure to wave goodbye and smile as we passed every single *viejos'* stall.

13

"Chau! Ya terminamos. Podes creer? Que horror!"

"Bye! We are done. Can you believe it? The horror!"

The *viejos* nodded and seethed. I could not wipe the grin off of my face. My mom had cut her teeth in a man's world and was not about to let these old men push her around. We made our way home and enjoyed the rest of our Wednesday.

...

Years later I would still be chomping at the bit to start another job or side hustle. If we made a good batch of *ñoquis* it was "ma, we could sell this." When my mother-in-law's hot oil livened up every dish it touched "Má, we should sell this!"

My mother would laugh at my half-cooked business plans. She was older now. Years of disease and hospitalizations had slowly chipped away at her vitality. Her hands were much too frail and shaky to work the overlock machine she had once presided over with such command.

"Ay nene, sos abogado. No tenès que estar dando vueltas con estas cosas tan chiquitas."

"Oh son, you're an attorney. You shouldn't be going in circles with these small things."

I had grown up and plowed ahead with my studies. I worked full time through college to pay my way. Studying, working and partying at a frenetic pace. I just now was realizing that what for me had become a central tenet for existence had been derived from my mom's survival tactics.

Hustling wasn't a way of life. It was a way to put food on the table. Sitting around the table and talking and laughing with your family? That was the way. Everything leading up to that was just a tool in the toolbox.

I am still learning to reframe how I think. Still seeing my own made up *viejos* in the distance and wanting to prove them wrong. I can rest securely, though, in knowing that if ever my career lags or times are tough I can always channel my inner flea market god and get right back at it...

"PANTALONES PANTAAAAALONES
Señorseñor pas páselepáselepásele elépaselépaselé!"

[hija]

It's a girl.

So they say:
Pink.
Flowers.
Pretty.
Dresses.
Shotguns.
Jokes!
Jokes?
Yes, I suppose.

But also:
Leader.
Divine.
Feminine as a superpower
and not a pejorative.
Boundless.
Funny.
Fearless.

The beauty of raising kids is that nobody really knows
what they are doing.
Our parents didn't.
Neither did our grandparents.

A long, winding generational trail
of "I think this"
And "let's try that?"

At some level you just lead by example.
They are always watching and observing.
You teach when teaching is needed
And listen when listening is the thing to do
And sometimes?
Sometimes you do nothing at all.
Just sit there and stare up at the clouds with them.

That one looks like a dragon.
This one looks like a tree.
That one looks like all the hopes and dreams
I have wrapped up in you growing
strong and smart and confident
and someday not needing us anymore
but sticking around because we share
blood and history and you have your mom's nose and my eyes
and the holidays wouldn't be the same without.

I will teach you what I know so far
like riding a motorcycle and cooking pasta
and learn what I need to learn,
like braiding hair and the math with the letters.

I loved you when you were just a dream of ours.

I love you now, a dream coming true.

And I'll love you far into the night sky when my last dream sweeps me away into the clouds.

Hasta pronto, mi Chiquitita.

[bully]

I got bullied by a kid named Dustin in 3rd grade. Classic pre-Internet bullied: Surreptitious elbows to the ribs, sweeping kicks to the ankles when walking single file to the lunchroom, whispered obscenities during class.

Dustin had me on edge. My social life up until that point had been idyllic, filled with street basketball, tag, and making games up with the neighborhood kids. In a matter of months, Dustin had undone all that.

Now I had to constantly look over my shoulder on the blacktop during recess. If I went to sip water from the drinking fountain, I had to ensure he was at least 20 ft away and not in range to smash my face into the water stream.

Dustin was a menace, a deceptive one at that. I saw it happen right before my eyes. He would lean in and whisper something dripping with meanness like "hey spic, your backs wet." The teacher would walk up and ask what we were chatting about. Dustin's face would morph in the second it took him to go from facing me to looking up at the teacher. His entire demeanor would change.

"Oh, sorry ma'am. I forgot my sharpener and I was asking Christian to borrow his."

The devious bastard.

I endured Dustin as much as possible. I fought back plenty, but he was a fair bit bigger than I was, and I would usually end up in

19

a headlock getting very unplayful noogies or on the ground with him in my half guard making me hit myself with my own hand.

[Years later I still don't know why I didn't tell a teacher or anyone at home. There was no street code in 4th grade to abide by. There were no gold stars for street cred.]

One day Dustin showed up to class with his arm in a cast. He had broken it at home, and it would be in a sling for the next 3 to 4 months. He stopped harassing me for a few days as he took in all the attention our classmates gave him because of his cast. Kids wanted to sign it and draw pictures all over it. That wore off soon enough and he went right back to making my life miserable.

Dustin tried to verbally bully me, but it wasn't as menacing when he didn't have the threat of physical violence behind it.

"Hey, idiot. Hey. Retard. I'm talking to you, you dumbshit."

I just ignored him.

...

My neighbor told me that when you get a cast taken off all the dead skin that has accumulated falls off as well and it stinks to high heaven. It had happened to her cousin over the summer and took weeks to finally smell better.

Bingo. That's all I needed to hear.

I could not get to school fast enough that next day. I ran out the door before I even finished chewing my breakfast. The walk to school was 11 blocks. That day it felt like two.

Before school kids would play on the blacktop and playground, waiting for the morning bell to ring. Usually there was one adult supervising, but it was impossible for them to cover the whole yard. I had to find the right moment to strike. I needed Dustin to be there but also a critical mass of other kids in our class had to be within earshot.

I waited around but Dustin didn't show up that day. He missed the following 3 days of school and my excitement waned. I did enjoy a nice respite from his aggression. Recess felt like a vacation. I played in the grassy field with the boys from other classes. We alternated between soccer, football and would almost always end up playing "Smear the Queer."

STQ consisted of one ball and an open field. There were no points, teams or real rules. Whoever had the ball was the enemy and you had to tackle him and strip the ball away. If you had the ball you ran for your life and tried not to get tackled. That was it. It now feels like a precursor to the mob mentality adults have when it comes to so many issues.

Years later I would realize how awful the name was and how the normalization of homophobia was everywhere. This was decades after Stonewall and Harvey Milk. Decades after we objectively should have known better, been more decent and human. How did this game keep getting handed down for generations in the school yard? Teachers and administrators must have known about it, right? It still boggles the mind.

For what it's worth, I asked my son and they still play this game at public schools but the name is long gone. Progress is glacial yet obstinate.

...

21

Dustin came back on Monday. The skin around his cheek and left eye had patches of green discoloration. The various stages of a bruise were playing out across his alabaster skin. He must have fallen or tried to bully someone he couldn't beat.

We got through the morning lessons without issue. The lunch bell rang, and we all lined up to walk to the cafeteria. Most of us received free lunch through the school program so we would walk single file to join the other classes and pick up our tray of food.

We ate at industrial 10-foot wooden picnic tables that could be wheeled in and out. During rainy days, the tables would be cleared out and the multi-purpose room would become a play area where we could get all of our energy out. As kids finished their lunch, they would put their trays in the designated area and congregate around the tables while waiting for the bell to ring.

I saw my opportunity. Dustin was still eating about 4 kids down and across from me and a large group had gathered around our table. I raised my voice and spoke to the back of the crowd.

"Hey guys, did you know that when you break your arm and it's in a cast that all your skin dies? Your skin dies and it keeps making more skin and the dead skin becomes mold and you stink."

"Naw-uh, for real?"

"Yeah man. Your arm stinks and it's hella dusty."

"Eewwwwwwww!" exclaimed one of the girls.

"I bet Dustin's arm stinks so bad! Oof, I can smell him from over here!" I shouted as I pinched my nose.

The trap was set Dustin looked around bewildered.

"That's not true" he yelled at the crowd. "I don't stink! My arm is fine!"

The crowd wasn't buying it. They had made their minds up. I had to close the deal.

"Dustin stinks so bad and I bet when they cut off his cast you won't even be able to see him. You'll just see a cloud of dust!"

Dustin's eyes widened as a group of girls laughed. He couldn't bully his way out of this one. I knew I had him beat. I could feel the crowd on my side. Revenge was exhilarating.

"HE'S DUSTY DUSTIN!!!" I proclaimed to the roar of the crowd. Fingers started pointing at him and chanting his new name. Dusty Dustin had nowhere to hide. His eyes started welling up with tears as he tried to appeal to the mob.

"What's the matter, Dusty Dustin? Got some dust in your eyes?" said a disembodied voice from the crowd. The mockery was flying in from all angles. Dusty Dustin grabbed his tray and stormed off, using his good arm to wipe away the tears.

The topic of conversation quickly changed, but the harm had been done. Dustin was Dusty Dustin for the rest of the school year. The hive mind was merciless. He stopped picking on me. He avoided me altogether.

My immediate lesson was that I may not be stronger than everyone, but I could always be wittier and there was power in that. I felt like I had wrestled back some sense of normalcy to my life.

Dustin's cast came off over the summer. No one ever got the lowdown on how dusty it may or may not have been. He was in my class the next year, but we sat at opposite ends of the classroom and hardly interacted. He was a terrible student and got sent to the principal's office often.

...

I remember one day riding my red and white Huffy bike home after school and deciding to take the long way home. I saw Dustin walking a few blocks ahead after I turned a corner. I slowed down a bit so I wouldn't catch up to him and saw him turn up a driveway into his house.

As I rode by, I saw beer cans strewn across their side yard and a broken-down Cabriolet in the driveway. The house was falling apart, and I could hear what sounded like yelling and arguing coming through the garage door. I rode by in silence and made my way home.

I don't remember much about Dustin after that. He either moved or was sent away, because he wasn't at our school after the holiday break, and I never saw him again.

...

I know now that Dustin was a broken boy. That he didn't actually hate me. He was hurt and flailing and mirroring all the pain and suffering he saw at home.

Now I recognize the broken bones, mysterious bruises, the many days missing from school without explanation and the wildly racist vocabulary for what they were: the symptoms of physical and verbal abuse. There was no way for me to understand all of that then. My home life was a dream at that age. It wasn't until a bit later that my parents would start arguing in earnest and I would have to reckon with my own trauma.

I wish I could have just grabbed Dustin by the shoulders and shaken him free. I wish I could have looked him in his pale blue eyes and reminded him that he is not his parents and that he is beautiful and smart and deserving of love. I wish I had the emotional maturity to recognize his pain and rather than hone in on it as a weakness, I had lifted him up.

You can't fix everybody. I know that. I know that my energy and time are limited, and I choose to focus on the ones that matter to me most. I also know that words are power, and people may forget what you did to them, but they'll never forget how you made them feel.

I hope Dustin is doing well. I hope he has shaken off the dust of his childhood trauma and mended his broken bones. I hope he's healed inside and out and that Dustin Jr. reaps the benefits of his pops doing the work it takes to get to that point.

Progress is glacial yet obstinate...

[water, water everywhere]

The ice on the windshield
is thick this morning.
The car shudders as I reach over
to blast the heat.

The birds are still tucked away
high up in their nests
dreaming, perhaps,
of winters further south
where windows never frost
and men are never broken.

The 805 is a parking lot.
We are collectively late,
dreams deferred,
as the chipper man on the radio
plays phone pranks
on the unsuspecting.

"Day after day, day after day,
We stuck, nor breath nor motion;
As idle as a painted ship
Upon a painted ocean."

> **the albatross swoops down low**
> **and glides towards the horizon**

There is no metaphor here.
There is only the albatross,
the traffic jam,
today
perhaps tomorrow
perhaps
perhaps

[invierno]

the winter of our discontent
ushers in the cold
the kind that creeps through
your thickest boots
claws through the wool layers
you thought could protect
and becomes your bones

your ego cracks
into a million shards of ice
the heart slows
to an uninspired tempo
keeping time with the
sullen shuffle of your frozen feet

gone are the bright summer mornings
with their wistful sunrises
gone are the birds
their joyous twittering
replaced with an icy silence
the trees no longer sway
in the languid breeze

the soil sleeps now
it knows to rest

and recover

it knows that the cold can only last for so long

and soon enough

the fingerlings of spring

will find their way through the melt

the tender tendrils tenacious

will grasp on and hold for dear life

the soil sleeps and waits

as we trudge on through the cold

and feed the embers of our memory

the tiny bits of summer we've left in us

[dando a luz]

I have seen your mother put in the work, child
hour after hour
breathing universes in through her nose

a low down moan
from deeper than I will ever understand
rumbling from her lips to the gods

a recitation of all the reasons she would die for you
a resuscitation of every single speck of stardust that makes her
wonderfully and fearfully
your Mother

I have seen our communities rally around us
lifting you up with their love and time and energy.

Generational wisdom
drip-dropping down to you
the knowledge of a long lineage of women
slowly filling the pools of your memory
bathing you in their light.

Welcome to the world, beloved.
It is full of love and exploration
dizzying heights and inconceivable lows.

We are here
to guide
and love
to help you treat glass ceilings like open doors
and dreams like future accomplishments.

We are here
with you
hasta el fin
mi mujercita divina.

Chiquitita

Lady Yen Vy

November 8th, 2020

1:42 AM

(mid)thirties

Papito,

Along the way you'll find a few good friends. Keep them close.

You'll hear a few good dirty jokes and lose some loved ones.
Remember them.

There will be nights you feel invincible, immortal even.
There will be days where every little bit of your heart aches, be it
for a woman, an ideal, or just because living can get to be so
damn hard sometimes.

Don't get too high. Don't get too low.

A good friend once told me all business is done in the margins.
Find the margins you feel at home in.

Get comfortable. You're gonna be there for a good while.

Remember that falling in love does not have to be a tempest.
It can be, but it doesn't have to be.

Ask more questions.
Demand more of others.
Demand more of yourself.

Just because this is the way adults do it now doesn't mean it's the way it needs to always be done.

Time is your biggest asset.

You are more than your job. More than your relationship status. More than your bank account. You are complex and nuanced and every facet of that fire within you deserves to burn bright. Do not allow anyone to ever make you feel otherwise.

It's OK to laugh at funerals.

There will be a few seminal moments in your life.

Ones where you will have a choice to make.

Or perhaps where all your loved ones will congregate to celebrate you in some manner.

Show up for those.

Be cognizant that it's happening and know that like everything else in this life, it, too, shall pass.

Learn the power of saying "no" early on.

Guard your heart.

Protect your siblings.

Spend more time than you think you'll need to with your parents.

Trust me on this one.

Once they're gone it will never seem like it was enough.

I love you.
I'm human and have made mistakes.
Surely I will make a few more.
But my love for you is unwavering and bright.
It is the closest I will ever come to eternity.

35 years is nothing and yet something.
We're all just walking each other home.
The morning light is just over the hill.
Let's enjoy this Now.

[this too shall pass]

This, too, shall pass
is not something an 8-month-old baby
understands
as these tiny bones
rip through her gums.

How could she know that?
The passage of time, much like these teeth,
is new to her.

Everything is new to her.

Wait until she finds out that we are but a speck of cosmic dust
hurtling through space
confined by laws of physics and time
mortal
sentient
beings
so engrossed in our wars and egos that we eventually
forget to look up and out into the night sky
and cry out in primal amazement and wide-eyed wonder.

What then, my love?
When this weeping and gnashing of teeth passes
and you are left to reckon with the rest of existence.

What then?

I intend to be here
Yet
To hold you
Close
And to love you
Still

And should I have moved
up and out,
through space and time,
look for me, love.
In the stars and in the quiet in-betweens.
Look for me
in the laughter that brings you to tears
and the tears that give way to laughter
and remember.

this, too, shall pass.

[morenita]

"She's so tan!"

"Shes looks like she spent a lot of time at the pool this summer."

[How many ways can you tell me my baby is dark?]

"She sure isn't afraid of the sun!"

"¡Mira que negrita que està!"

**How many ways can you find to throw
your complexes onto her complexion?**

"You got some color on you!"

"She matches her Padres shirt."

**This is Mapuche blood. These are Quechua tones. These are the
hues that survived genocides (plural) and resisted and
persisted.**

"She's going to tan soooooo well when she grows up!"

"I love how much caramel she has in her skin!"

This is General Roca's "Conquest of the Desert" gone wrong.
These are the Argentine Pampas and Chilean Andes and every
soul song that drives roots deep and wide into the soil.

This is an unabashed love song to the Vietnamese fishing boats
and Argentine boleadoras. You cannot contour your face nor
contort your history to match the heart and soul of

this little baby girl.

This is a sense of Self that drives deep into us and is not
defined by your odd fixation of looking like us in your
touched-up magazines but not standing by us when they
mowed us down, pushed and prodded, and (in what can only
be the most cosmic of ironies) eventually had us doing the
mowing.

This is a Sisyphean chip on my shoulder
that she will not be handed down.

This is a warning shot.

This is a brown-skinned snarl and showing of teeth.

"¡Wow, qué prieta!"

"No pos, si estábien morenita, no?"

...and so on and so forth...

[naptime]

I can feel your breath.
Tiny gasps against my chest
trembling from the sobs.
Air thick with tears and sputtered supplications
to stay up just a little longer.

I am not asking you to lay here
prostrated in somnambulant prayer
to a sleep god you evidently do not believe in
for my own good.

You need this.
WE need this.

I am tired and covered in boogers and tears.
The sound machine plays an endless ocean.
You radiate heat.

You are my tiny, godless furnace.

You are the altar and the priest and the volcano.
I am the lamb
quietly bleating out lullabies
rhythmically rocking towards redemption.

"Amazing grace... how sweet the sound..."

[late to the party]

We are late to the party.

(I could tell you about how the undulating hills in Temecula
cause a daily traffic backup and how, after years of going back
and forth to pick up my now 15-year-old son, I wish they'd blow
those damn hills to hell, but that's beside the point.)

We are late to the party.

We are headed to a friend's surprise birthday and on the way I
notice the address we were given is residential. The house is atop
a hill that overlooks the entire bay. The twinkling lights below
and the reflections from the ocean make the sky seem endless; the
possibilities limitless.

The house itself is a work of art. An oversized door swings open
much easier than it physically should, defying the laws of
physics. The mix of glass, wood and steel is an affront to the
elements; a stake in the ground daring the gods or the veritable
big bad wolf to even try it.

I pull on the door and we see the party: it's an old-fashioned
dinner party. The visages of friends and strangers alike smile at
us as we enter awkwardly and try our best to assimilate to the
vibe which had already been established.

I sit at the perfectly manicured table and take it all in. The hosts
seated next to us are a kind couple. After the wine starts flowing
a bit I learn that he was a museum curator and his father was a

big cattle ranch owner in Texas. Later in the evening, he would go on to show me around his home museum, picking up a 2,000-year-old ceramic dog/grain holder from Ixtapa with his bare hands and joyfully pointing out some of the intricate details.

"This is Venice from the Venusian period in 1799," he says pointing to a large oil on canvas. I nod and feign understanding.

"This is a Goya," he says, pointing to a smaller frame with a sketch of some sort.

"Like the beans?" I think to myself but refrain from saying out loud. Maybe it would get a laugh but also probably it would not.

The evening is a fine waltz between creating memories with dear friends and trying not to tip my hand as to how poor I grew up while seated next to Mr. Curator. The personal chef comes from the kitchen to explain the intricacies of each course; everyone nods and feigns understanding.

My mom once told me how she would go to the grocery store when they first moved here from Argentina and she only had a few dollars for the week's groceries. My older sister, 11 then, wanted some yogurt. My mom knew she could not afford it if she wanted to keep everyone fed until next payday. She swore then and there that she would do whatever it takes to make sure her daughter could have yogurt whenever she damn well pleased.

I think about that little girl and her yogurt as I stare down at the decadent dessert before me which, I learned 5 seconds ago, had been created by a French noble for a Russian diplomat way back in the days when either still existed. I think about the vastly different worldviews that little girl necessarily would have from Mr. Curator.

I think about how I had to work full time while in college to make ends meet and how the only reason I know how to eat with this plethora of utensils is because of that dinner party scene in the movie *Titanic* and how our gracious host has probably never had to think about any of these things.

I think about how I can buy all the yogurt I want and how I don't even like yogurt. I think about how no amount of yogurt would buy me this beautiful house with its boundless views or afford me the life where I could choose a career like museum curation to begin with.

I think about how we have a seat at the table but it's not our table and not our house...

and we are late to the party.

[mondaze]

It is always Monday.
On that, at the very least, we can most certainly count on.

The years peel off
one by one
as we chip away to get to the core
of who and why we are.

Some Mondays are birthdays.
Others anniversaries.
Some Mondays languish from wanting
while others are technicolored dreamcoated orgasms of activity.

My youngest pecks away at her breakfast dutifully and has not a
clue what day it might be.
For her, it is always now.
If she wants something, it is now.
If she loves you, it is now.
If she is sleepy or hungry or cuddly, it is now.

Her smile is now and her tears are now.
Now is eternal and there is no time to waste on naming the days.
At most, days are used to delineate what the letter of the day will
be on *Sesame Street*.

The letter of the day today is M.
M is for Monday.

[La PooPee]

My dog follows me from room to room as I putter around throughout my day. I work from home and spend much of my day going back and forth from the home office to the kitchen. A glass of water, maybe some almonds, a fresh cup of coffee. On occasion I will sit on the couch and listen to a song or part of a podcast. A nap is had from time to time, usually with the windows open to allow for a breeze to blow in. My dog will nestle all 12 lbs. of herself against me any time I lay down. She is faithful and kind, albeit a bit stupid from time to time.

My wife likes to say she is a rescue dog whenever people ask where we got her from.

"Oh, we rescued her."

She is not lying, but then again, I don't think the term "rescue" is absolute. We had been wanting a dog for some time. More enamored, perhaps, with the idea of a dog and not so much the daily possessing of said dog. At various points in our 9 years together, a dog was offered to us or we had our (literal) pick of the litter. It never felt right and therefore never came to be.

My mother had been sick for some time and I had to drive up from San Diego to Bakersfield to meet my brother half way and help in transporting my ailing mother from Sacramento down to my sister's house in Riverside. (Yes, that is a lot of California cities to rattle off, and no, you do not need to know where any of those are, save to simply understand that I had about a 10 hour round trip on my hands to pick my mother up and drop her off at my sister's house.)

As they pulled into the Taco Bell parking lot where we had agreed to meet, I saw that my uncle Rolando had tagged along for the ride. Rolando is the youngest of my living uncles and thoroughly blue collar. He looks like a squinty, Latino version of Rodney Dangerfield. Much like his Caucasian doppelganger, Rolando thought he did not get enough respect from the world at large.

As Rolando lowered himself out of my brother's truck, his broad shoulders blocking out the neon glow from the "Live Mas" sign, I embraced my brother and checked on my mom. My mom was a resilient woman. She had flourished out of what some would refer to as "humble beginnings" but, if we are going to be clinical, we would identify as debilitating poverty, institutionalized misogyny and sexual abuse.

My mom was not simply a survivor, she was a leader who had lived her entire life intent on not allowing anybody, man or woman, to dominate her in a public nor private sphere. She was a lioness with her words and her actions. I was born after she immigrated to the United States and even then, a foreigner in strange lands, I saw her spirit triumph, over and over. She was always the hardest worker in the room, the loudest voice with the boldest opinion. That was my mom for me most of my life and here we were, now, in a darkened parking lot trying to transfer her over comfortably and without bruising her.

She had spent the last six years getting progressively sicker from a genetic blood disorder causing issues with her liver and then her heart and then her kidneys. The fire in her eyes remained as the rest of her withered away slowly. The weight loss, at first a welcome side effect as she had spent years drinking dieter's teas or trying one fad diet or another to lose those last obstinate kilos, had now consumed her almost entirely. Her face sank low and when I would help her change her shirt I could see every single bone and juncture in her spine.

As we settled in for the long ride I started asking questions about the puppy my Tio Rolando had brought. Her name was "Puppy" but said like "Poo-Pee" in the most typical of Latino fashion. Rolando's dog had a litter, and this was the last one that no one seemed to want. Rolando was taking it down to one of my mom's friends since she had expressed interest in another dog.

"Do you like it?" my mom asked. This was one of her lucid days. She would go through phases where she was her old self, mentally aware and inquisitive, and then other phases where she would be a bit lost or even child-like. There was even a spell where she only spoke English to us. My mother, the strong proponent of a Spanish-only household who had spent years scolding us for speaking anything but Spanish in her presence, spent a full three days responding with "What? What do you mean? I am no sick. I am good and this noorse does not want to make my soup hot. I no eat cold soup." (Note that even in her altered mind states she was bossing people around and demanding things be served to her approval.)

"I do like it. *Està muy bonita la perrita.*" I responded. By this point I had already sent a picture to my wife with the caption, "Isn't she cute?"

"If you like it, you should keep it."

"No Mamita, I can't. Rolando already promised it to your friend."

51

"That was not Rolando's dog to give away! He offered that dog to me, and I said I wanted it. Then your sister said I was too sick to have a dog."

"But you are sick mami..."

"I don't care if I'm sick! That is MY dog and no one has ANY RIGHT to give it away to ANYBODY. If you want that dog you can have that dog!" The volume of my mom's voice had diminished considerably over the years but the fiery timbre remained.

"What about your friend?"

"So. What. That is my dog. I will call her right now. Where is my phone?"

"Ma, it's late."

"So? *Las cuentas claras*." She would always use that phrase which translates to "clear accounts" as a stanchion for how she chose to live her life: clearly and with no confusion. Her bookkeeping, like her friendships and her love, were always clear and direct and absent any gray area. She either loved you dearly or did not have time for you. In much the same way, she had no time to waste with what ifs and perhaps not.

Ring. Ring.

"*Hola amiga*! Yes, I am on the road. Listen, I know that Rolando had promised you that dog but that dog was given to me first and I am going to keep it.

I waited in silence as the highway rumbled below us.

"Yes, I know I am sick. You don't have to tell me I am sick. I know I am sick, but that doesn't matter. You don't need to worry about how I will take care of the dog. I just want to let you know that I am keeping it. I am sorry, but that is the way it is going to be.

"Ok, yes, we will see you tomorrow. Chau."

Just like that I was the owner of a brand new (to me) PooPee. That was my mother in a nutshell. Healthy or sick, she was always true to herself and what she believed in. She was unrelenting in her loyalty to those that she loved. Social norms be damned. If her *chiquito* wanted the puppy and it was going to take a difficult conversation for him to have it, then that was a conversation she would have without hesitation.

I dropped my mom and Rolando off at my sister's house and headed home. The puppy slept in the passenger seat and I stared off into the undulating hills the 15 freeway takes you through to get back down to San Diego. I was 32 and had a wife and a son, a career and an ailing mother. Now I was adding a small dog to the mix.

...

My mom passed away on October 1st, 2018 in my sister's living room the same day we had put her on hospice care. She had fought very long and had strongly voiced her opinion against

53

hospice care for years. Her past jobs had included taking care of elderly clients in hospice and she saw firsthand how the overuse of morphine and other medications stole the light away from them. My mother guarded her light to the very end. That last night she had spent the entire night struggling to breathe, the fluids in her body weighing too heavily on her lungs and not allowing her to take full breaths. She knew that the only way to get an oxygen tank for her was to put her on hospice care and she gave my sister her consent.

The oxygen tank came in the morning and gave her some relief. She promptly fell asleep, and we started making preparations for what we felt was the inevitable. The siblings spoke and we made plans in terms of days and even weeks. We thought we had more time.

I had my back turned to her as I finished some work on my laptop at the counter. She had been sleeping the entire afternoon/evening and there was an uneasy calm in the house. The pastor from the local Spanish church and his wife had spent the evening with us. I learned that sharing in the hard times is as much a part of that profession as celebrating the good ones.

I heard a commotion behind me and my sister, a medical doctor, exclaimed "This is not good." As I ran around to the other side of the bed, I saw my mom's eyes wide open and staring towards the ceiling. The last embers were blowing out. It was happening now.

I grabbed her hand as she convulsed slightly. Her mouth was partially open and her eyes were glazing. I pressed my head against hers and started saying "I'm sorry" over and over, apologizing for what I'm not sure. Perhaps for all the times we argued or for the times I made her cry. Perhaps because I wasn't in charge of Time and couldn't give her more.

I'm sorry. I'm sorry. I'm sorry.

My sister ran to get her stethoscope off the counter as the pastor started wailing. He came from a long line of Latinos where death is to be met with loud crying and emotion. His wife started praying out loud. They had seen this scene before and knew what to do. I had not and did not. My vision narrowed and I just held her hand and pressed my face against her. I asked for forgiveness, begged for it, over and over and over. From her, from God perhaps. I asked that this hurt stop hurting. I asked that Death be held at bay at least for a little longer because I wasn't done being a boy and I wasn't done needing my Mamita.

The children cried. The grandchildren cried. The in-laws cried. PooPee ran back and forth, confused and wanting to provide some type of love and affection. Perhaps just wanting attention. She is faithful and kind, albeit a bit stupid from time to time.

...

My dog follows me from room to room as I putter around throughout my day. Most of my time is spent preoccupied but I still get hit with these waves of emotion that crash into me and slowly subside into the whitewater of my memories. I miss my Mamita. I carry her with me, from room to room, from memory to memory. She is in the way I make my decisions, the pastas that I crave, the manner in which I choose to show my love and affection. She follows me, from room to room, reminding me to

55

be faithful and kind and that it is ok to be a bit stupid from time to time.

[one]

I thought I had loved in all the ways possible.

young love

growing old love

broke-and-can-barely-make-rent-but-we-know-we-got-each-other love

the kind of love that follows the moonrise

and disappears with the sun

a father's love

a brother's love

the love you feel when everyone you love is under one roof

[happy and healthy and alive]

and you can't imagine your heart filling up with any more love than what it currently has.

I thought I had loved every way my heart and mind would allow.

I had written about it and sung songs about it, had happy hour become happy hours about it and cried about it.

I thought I knew the depths and the limits of my love.

That the heartbreaks I had felt were the mirrored valleys to the peaks of my potential to love.

I know, now, that none of that is true.

I know now that the only limit to my love is my own capacity to imagine it.

That a second child does not take half from the same well as the first

But that they get their own well, deep and ever-flowing, from which to draw my love

…

I know that today you turn one

And tomorrow you will turn 30.

That my mom always told me her life felt like the blink of an eye

And at 12 I could not possibly understand what she meant

But at 36 I can't imagine it any other way.

I know that you are loved by me and your mom and your brother

and this myriad of concentric social circles we have built along the way.

I know that we hold you up, in love and positivity,

on this day and every day thereafter.

I know that I see in you the boundless potential to love

and be loved

And for that I thank you and want to wish you

a very happy birthday, mi *chiquitita*.

[frida calvo]

My wife leaves me small works of art in the shower.
Hair is her preferred medium.

Every morning is a Rorschach test
as I turn the faucet and wait for the warm water to make its way
through the pipes.

The strands swoop around and intersect each other at sharp
angles.
They defy gravity
plastered up against the tiles by the humidity.
They defy god.

I am no art critic. Far be it for me to judge her process or question
the truth behind her artistic vision.

I am just a man.
In a shower.
Standing before a hairball.

And if the true meaning of art is to evoke emotion
then these are a compendium of daily masterpieces.

They initially evoked annoyance but through their persistent
presence over the years they now bring up a fondness rooted in
familiarity.

They tell a story across time. Their lengths and color belie the seasons of our life. The stresses of career and motherhood affect their volume. [The Postpartum Period was prolific.]

It's Bauhaus with balayage.

Umbra via ombré.

A Louvre of love, if you will.

I feel water cascade down my back as I lather shampoo on my head.

I breathe in deeply and exhale as the vanity mirror begins to fog up.

Today's piece slowly starts to slide down the tile towards the drain.

Tomorrow is another day.

[terror dactyls]

my toes do not wriggle like yours, my love

in fact
they do not wriggle at all.

they sidle up next to each other
like friends at a bar
shoulder to shoulder
beer in hand
tuned in to a third-rate soccer league
waiting for something exciting to happen.

my toes do not fan open like a cockatoo's tail
and lift objects 10 times their size.

[I do not have Solange's phalanges]

My toes will not win any awards
nor pay for your tuition
with what I may make on OnlyFeet.

Abuela always said I had *"pata de indio"* and *"pata de pobre"*
which means Abuela was vaguely racist and classist
when it came to toes.

There is no ending here, dear.

I can give you my name

but I'm glad you got your mama's toes.

[chasing sunsets]

You turned two today.
Your mother and I are chasing the sunset
making our way back to you.
(The closest I will ever get to time travel.)

On the airport shuttle in Reykjavik
I saw an older Indian mom
laying into her adult son
about some trivial issue.

She spoke hurriedly in her dialect
but as a former adult son myself
I could tell he was getting the business.

The son brushed her off in such an off-handed way that belied his
decades of experience dealing with her.

He deftly placed one of his earbuds in and pressed play as his
mom continued her diatribe. The son and I made eye contact and
he flashed me a pained grimace.

Oh, to be yelled at by your Abuela again!
Behold the power of absence
that even the sound of her *gritos* is missed over time.

I tell you all this to say that I know you will tire of me someday.

63

and that you and your mother
will most assuredly clash
over and over and over.

I can see even now that your anger
burns white hot like hers
and I know your tiny teenage heart
full of hormones and passion
will feel wronged many times over.

Remember it all,
mi Chiquitita,
lo bueno y lo malo.

I am doing what I can to remember you
as you are now.
Two years old.
Bright eyes and strong opinions.
To remember your gleeful giggles and the way you tuck your
arms into my chest on cold mornings when we walk out to the
car.

I would chase every sunset to be with you.
Feliz cumpleaños, mi nena querida.

[una paliza]

I was ready to beat my children
at the first sign of dissent.
To impose my will upon them
by force if necessary.
To sternly say "go get the wooden spoon"
and they would know
I meant the wooden spoon we use to stir the bottom
of the simmering sauce pan
when making ragu.

They would cry, sob even,
and I would have to choose
to stand there stoic like my father
or rant and yell like my mother
as I applied the mechanical violence,
bereft of emotion,
and tell them repeatedly this was hurting me more than it hurt
them.

The stinging crack of the wood
punctuated by their yelps and yips
was to be the symphonia of their moral education.

I was fully prepared to pass down
the brutality

handed to me

palm by palm

and bathe in the crescendo of righteousness that would surely accompany it.

...

Sometimes we get so used to the weight of our burdens
we forget they are even there.

Sometimes our blind spots are so vast
they become the only thing we can see.

...

My 2-year-old hands a red ball of Play-Doh to my 15-year-old.

She asks him to build her a snowman.

He slowly starts rolling out the base for a strong foundation.

He is peaceful and she is chaos.

Their energies meet somewhere in the middle; she squeals with delight as he adds a tiny top hat to the snowman.

I take the lid off the saucepan and stir with my wooden spoon. The one only known as the ragu spoon in this house.

"Dinner is ready. *A comer!*"

[ready or not]

around the time
my eldest found out about girls
my youngest found out about boogers.

how to explain to them
that it is natural
but there are rules
to what you should and should not do
with girls and boogers?

that you can pick your own boogers
but should not pick someone else's

that your booger may taste good
but you probably shouldn't eat it,
especially not in public,
and definitely don't mash it down
into the sheets
or play with its feelings.

that booger has hopes and dreams
too
you know?

[That booger deserves your best intentions.]

my third is on the way.
he too will find out
about girls and boogers
someday

hopefully by then
we are stocked up on tissue
and are a bit more ready
to hold this space for him
to explore and pick at his own pace.

[the last of us]

There is a baby in there,
mi Chiquitita.

You, too, were in there once.

I watched your mother's discomfort grow
as you tossed and turned
right jab to the bladder
left cross for good measure.

I held you in one hand
right up to my face
and worried that my breath was too hot
or that if my eyes stared too much
you would get the *mal de ojo*
the *brujas* of my childhood
always talked about.

I marveled
(I marvel still)
at your ability to be so tiny
yet carry the weight of my love
with you everywhere you go.

I counted your fingers and toes

69

over and over

undostrescuatrocincoseissieteochonuevediez

over and over

as if my brain

did not want to take my heart's word for it

that you are perfect.

There is a baby in there,

mi Chiquitita,

and he will be here soon

with us

(One of us)

You will need to help him shoulder

the weight of our hearts

beating outside our bodies

and help him know that mama and papá

are not fighting at the dinner table

we are just passionately recounting

what that *idiota* from accounting said to us

earlier.

You will need to grow old with him

and laugh with him

and someday cry with him

once your mama and papá are gone.

For now we wait
and marvel
together
at the tiny footprint bulging from
your mother's taut belly.

[tiny blue shards]

When I was 12 or so my mom took me on a trip with my sister
and future brother-in-law around Europe. She had spent years in
the immigrant struggle, fighting to pave her own way in a foreign
land and it was finally paying some dividends. My mom was
thriving and she wanted to explore.

I have a hundred stories from that trip. Like the one where I
snuck out of the hotel in Paris on the night my sister got engaged
and caught my first punk show at a coffee shop or how my CD
disc holder was stolen and I was only left with a copy of Ricky
Martin's 1998 Grammy Award Winning album *Vuelve* to listen to
over and over again as we trained from country to country. Most
hear a Ricky Martin song and want to shake their bon bon but I
can clearly see the train station signage in Versailles and feel the
click clack of the train as it lurches forward over the tracks.

Livin' la vida loca, indeed.

That summer was magic and like any magical story, it had to
have a villain. My villain was three pieces of blue Murano crystal
my mom bought in Venice on one of our first days out. There
were two ornate vases and a large dish made out of this much
storied glass which was hand blown and etched with gold. My
mom was hooked on all the narratives, and she had to buy these.
Simply. Had to.

Some of my memories are faint. I remember the touristy must of
Rome and the languid canals of Venice. I remember a day spent
in Montecarlo. The loud, exotic cars on the avenue and opulent
buildings hewn into the hard mountainside at the water's edge

72

screaming out "Look at us and how we laugh in the face of nature and God herself!"

Some memories are so vivid I can still feel the weight of them in my hand. We marched those three glass pieces in their Styrofoam and tape sarcophaguses all through Europe. On the train. Off the train. Into the hotel. Out of the hotel. Another train. Another country. The same damned bulky bag just dragging me down, over and over.

Europe at 12 years old was a fever dream. I saw the Mona Lisa up close. I lugged that glass around. I climbed the Eiffel Tower. I hoisted those vases into another tiny Citroen taxi. Sometimes we stayed in one hotel just long enough that I forgot that bag of fancy glass even existed. Without fail at checkout time they would poke their gold-plated head out from under the bed and scream "WE ARE YOUR BURDEN FOREVERMORE!"

I had more than one argument with my mom about that glass. How she shouldn't have bought it. How she should be the one to lug it around if she loved it so much. She was obstinate in her enthusiasm. No pre-teen *pendejito* was going to make her second guess her purchase.

Once we arrived home she unwrapped her prized pieces and displayed them in the dining room. There they stayed. Years rolled by. Births. Birthdays. Graduations. Weddings. Around the table we gathered. To eat and argue and laugh. Wrinkles deepened. Decades passed. Slowly we all moved away and began to recreate our own versions of those long family meals.

73

The Murano perdured. The pieces would get dusty and my mom would clean them off. They would be moved out of harm's way for big events and always put back on display after. My memories of how much I hated lugging them around during that hot summer trip slowly faded into the recesses of my memory.

...

My mom died slow, in her own time. She repeatedly defied all expectations, willed herself beyond the bounds of nature. She was the Monte Carlo of senior citizens.

She left behind lots of things. A lifetime's worth of things. Objects from daily life, keepsakes from her travels. Those damned Murano pieces. At one point I took the two vases home and my brother held on to the dish. Not because we wanted them, necessarily, but just because they needed to go somewhere. I meant to go drop them off at my sister's house eventually but instead I placed the vases on a shelf next to a happy Buddha in the kitchen and there they sat. For years. Gathering dust and watching us as we went about our lives.

...

A few weeks ago I went to install a doggie entrance on the side door to our house. The dog had been waking us up to go out and pee and I had finally had enough. Armed with a few power tools and a bit of patience I set about my work. I hummed my favorite Argentine folk song as I measured and re-measured before drilling.

"Zamba de mi esperanza

There is a certain amount of peace and satisfaction that comes with creating something with your hands.

"Sueño, sueño del alma

Que a veces muere sin florecer"

As I drilled through the door, focused gaze on my guiding line, I heard it. Above the din of the jig saw it rang out. One loud crash. A beautiful cacophony as a thousand tiny shards exploded all over the kitchen. I felt it sting across the back of my leg as it detonated. It looked like a tiny Italian craftsman had snuck in to engage in a specific kind of guerrilla warfare that only used expertly crafted glass hand grenades.

I cried. Out of frustration. Out of anger. Out of a realization that one more tie that kept my memory of my mom close to me had snapped and I was left holding all these tiny shards of her and wishing that I could have just held it all together one more time. Wishing I could have held her hand again and walked all through Europe and not complained about the weight of that bag and not have spent so many hours on the train staring off into the distance listening to shitty pop music and rather have turned to her and asked her more questions. Learned more about her. From her.

...

I swept and wiped down the countertop in silence. Aidan and Lan followed suit. They knew about that damned Murano and knew it meant nothing but also meant a lot. We cleaned every nook and cranny, vacuumed and re-vacuumed. We slowly picked up the pieces.

"El tiempo que va pasando
Como la vida no vuelve más
El tiempo me va matando
Y tu cariño será, será"

[the sum of us]

where there was one
now four
and soon
five

the calculus changes
every time

car seat configurations
divisions of labor
your heart somehow making space
exponentially

once again
surrounded by love
once again
with the tiny baby shoes
that are so impossibly small you can't imagine a foot to fit it
once again
we find the sum of all the love
we give is returned to us a hundredfold

[Jorah]

there is a C-section taking
place next door

I can hear everything
the beeps of the heart
monitor syncopating the
light and airy conversation
of the cutter and the drugger

they are playing the Doobie Brothers
on the speaker
or maybe it's *Aja* by Steely Dan
it is hard to tell over the clanging
of instruments and the constant beeping

they will name him Jorah
which means first rain
says the mother as she waits
for the drugs to kick in
and her insides to come out

a mother's love
knows no bounds
but I do so wish
that someone would tell

Jorah's mom that
Taking It To The Streets
should never be
the first song you listen to
nor the last.

[gone fishin']

the crashing waves give way to calm
the further you go out to sea.

The horizon stretches forever,
eventually,
and you're left with your thoughts
and some beers
and some conversation.

The hours pass methodically
as the captain scours the radar
for flashes of blue and yellow
like a miner staring deep into a pan of sandy water.

> *Bluefin come up to eat when it's hot.*
> *Sea lions will snap your mackerel bait in half to avoid the hook.*
> *Kelp patties make for good fishing.*
> *Bananas? Don't you dare bring those on board.*

Fishing is a long list of rules and superstitions
you learn by osmosis.
Maybe none of it matters.
Maybe all of it does.

You can fight a bluefin for an hour,

reeling him in on the way up.

giving him slack on the way out.

Back and forth,

a game of leverage and speed on both ends.

The fish will run when it sees the boat clearly.

It will shoot down to the depths

into the dark unknown of the vast ocean beneath your feet.

somethings gotta give

the fish

the line

the hook

You

On the way back to the docks

the seagulls and sea lions follow closely,

waiting for the deckhands to throw over

some guts or a fish head.

You learned a bit more.

Either you caught a fish or you didn't.

Your nose is a bit burnt

and the ocean air has misted everything with salt.

The sun dips below the horizon

and in the penumbra

you carry your load
up the dock
and into the night.

Principito

River Hai
February 13, 2023
3:05 PM

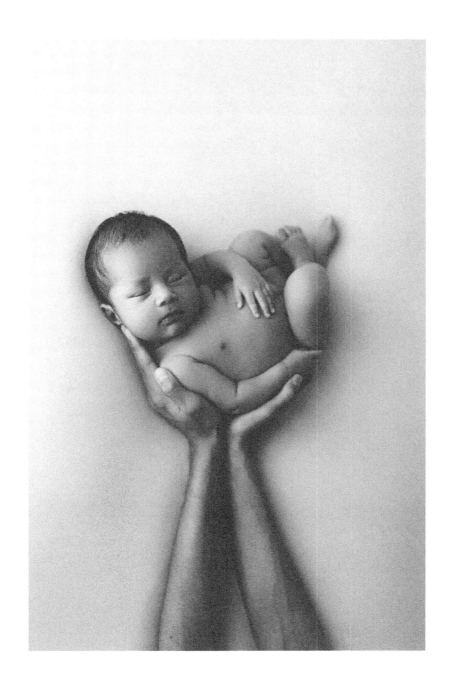

C.G MORO is a poet-cum-attorney based in San Diego, CA. He has published three chapbooks: *20 years of Solitude y una cancion desperada* (2006), *The Kid Falls* (2008), and *30 Years a Fool* (2015). His work explores the fatherhood dynamic, the immigrant experience from the perspective of a second-generation immigrant and tacos as a metric for gentrification.

Made in the USA
Monee, IL
19 October 2023

44794774R00059